The Runaway Pancake

First published in the United States by
Larousse & Co., Inc.
572 Fifth Avenue
New York, N.Y. 10036
1980
Reprinted 1981, 1984

This edition first published in Denmark
by Gyldendalske Boghandel
as *Pandekagen* in 1980

Originally published in 1871 as 'Pannekaken' in
Norske Folke-Eventyr, a collection of Norwegian folk
tales

Illustrations Copyright © 1980 Svend Otto S.
English Translation Copyright © 1980 Pelham
Books Ltd

ISBN 0-88332-137-8
Library of Congress Catalog Card No. 80-80439
Printed in Denmark

P. CHR. ASBJØRNSEN AND JØRGEN MOE

The Runaway Pancake

Illustrated by Svend Otto S.

Translated by Joan Tate

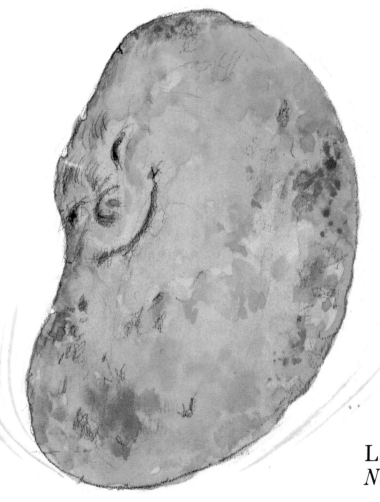

Larousse & Co., Inc.
New York

Once upon a time, there was a woman who had seven hungry children. She was making a pancake for them, with egg and milk and flour. It lay there in the pan, all bubbly and thick, with all the children standing round and Grandfather looking on.

"Oh, give me a little piece of pancake, Mother," said one of the children. "I'm so hungry."

"Oh, Mother dear," said the second.

"Oh, dear kind Mother," said the third.

"Oh, dear kind good Mother," said the fourth.

"Oh, dear beautiful kind good
Mother," said the fifth.

"Oh, dear beautiful kind good
clever Mother," said the sixth.

"Oh, dear beautiful kind good
clever sweet Mother," said the
seventh.

They all begged for a piece of pancake, each one of them even more sweetly than the last, because they were all so hungry.

"Yes, yes, children," she said. "Just wait until it turns over" – until I turn it over, she should have said – "then you will all have a piece. Just look how fat and contented it looks."

When the pancake heard this, it was frightened, and in a flash turned itself over and tried to get out of the pan. But it fell back again on to its other side. When it had fried a little on that side, too, so that it was firmer, it leapt out on to the floor and rolled away like a wheel, through the door and down the road.

"Hey, stop!" cried Mother, and away she went after it with the pan in one hand and the ladle in the other. The children ran after her, with Grandfather limping along behind.

"Hey, stop! Stop it! Catch it!" they all
shouted at once, trying to catch up with it.
But the pancake rolled on and on and on.
Then suddenly it had rolled right out of
sight, for the pancake was faster than any
of them.

When it had rolled on for a while
it met a man.

"Good-day, pancake," said the
man.

"God bless, Manny-Panny," said
the pancake.

"Pancake, dear, please don't roll
so fast," said the man. "Stop for a
while and let me eat you up."

"As I've managed to escape from Mother-Puther, Grandfather and seven squealing children, then I might as well escape from you, Manny-Panny," said the pancake, rolling on until it met a hen.

"Good-day, pancake," said the hen.

"Good-day, Henny-Penny," said the pancake.

"Pancake, dear, please don't roll so fast," said the hen. "Stop for a while and let me eat you up."

"As I've managed to escape from Mother-Puther, Grandfather, seven squealing children, and from Manny-Panny, then I might as well escape from you, Henny-Penny," said the pancake, rolling on down the road like a wheel.

Then it met a rooster.

"Good-day, pancake," said the rooster.

"Good-day, Rooster-Pooster," said the pancake.

"Pancake, dear, please don't roll so fast," said the rooster. "Stop for a while and let me eat you up."

"As I've managed to escape from Mother-Puther, Grandfather, seven squealing children, from Manny-Panny and Henny-Penny, then I might as well escape from you, Rooster-Pooster," said the pancake, rolling on as fast as it could.

When it had rolled along for a long long time, it met a duck.

"Good-day, pancake," said the duck.

"Good-day, Ducky-Lucky," said the pancake.

"Pancake, dear, please don't roll so fast," said the duck. "Stop for a while and let me eat you up."

"As I've managed to escape from Mother-Puther, Grandfather, seven squealing children, from Manny-Panny, Henny-Penny and Rooster-Pooster, then I might as well escape from you, Ducky-Lucky," said the pancake, rolling on faster than ever.

When it had rolled along for a long long time, it met a goose.

"Good-day, pancake," said the goose.

"Good-day, Goosey-Poosey," said the pancake.

"Pancake, dear, please don't roll so fast," said the goose. "Stop for a while and let me eat you up."

"As I've managed to escape from Mother-Puther, Grandfather, seven squealing children, from Manny-Panny, Henny-Penny, Rooster-Pooster and from Ducky-Lucky, then I might as well escape from you, Goosey-Poosey," said the pancake, rolling away again.

When it had rolled on for a long long
time, it met a gander.

"Good-day, pancake," said the gander.

"Good-day, Gander-Pander," said the
pancake.

"Pancake, dear, please don't roll so
fast," said the gander. "Stop for a while
and let me eat you up."

"As I've managed to escape from
Mother-Puther, Grandfather, seven
squealing children, from Manny-Panny,
Henny-Penny, Rooster-Pooster,
Ducky-Lucky and from Goosey-Poosey,
then I might as well escape from you,
Gander-Pander," said the pancake, rolling
on faster and faster.

When it had rolled on for a long
long time, it met a pig.

"Good-day, pancake," said the
pig.

"Good-day, Piggy-Wiggy," said
the pancake, rolling on even faster.

"Hey, not so fast," said the pig. "We two
can keep each other company through the
forest. They say it's not very safe in there."
The pancake thought there was
something in that, so off they went.

After a while, they came to a stream.
The pig floated across, without any
difficulty, because of all his fat, but the
pancake couldn't get across.

"You sit on my snout," said the pig.
"And I'll carry you across." So the
pancake did.

"Sshloomph," said the pig, gobbling
the pancake down in one great gulp.
And as the pancake got no further,
this story is no longer.